Eerie Elementary

The Locker ATE Lucy!

By Jack Chabert
Illustrated by Sam Ricks

BRANCHES

SCHOLASTIC INC.

5/18

READ ALL THE
Eerie Elementary
ADVENTURES!

MORE BOOKS
COMING SOON!

TABLE OF CONTENTS

For my Mom. Love ya! — JC

Library of Congress Cataloging-in-Publication Data

Chabert, Jack, author.
The locker ate Lucy! / by Jack Chabert.
pages cm. — (Eerie Elementary ; 2)
Summary: Only a week into his job as hall monitor and class protector, Sam Graves and his friends Lucy and Antonio are trying to uncover the secrets of Eerie Elementary, their living and malevolent school — and then Lucy gets eaten by her locker.
ISBN 0-545-62395-2 (pbk. : alk. paper) — ISBN 0-545-62396-0 (hardcover : alk. paper) — ISBN 0-545-62397-9 (ebook) 1. Elementary schools — Juvenile fiction. 2. Best friends — Juvenile fiction. 3. Rescues — Juvenile fiction. 4. Horror tales. [1. Schools—Fiction. 2. Best friends—Fiction. 3. Friendship — Fiction. 4. Rescues — Fiction. 5. Horror stories.] I. Title.
PZ7.C3313Lo 2014
813.6 — dc23
2013046259
ISBN 978-0-545-62396-4 (hardcover)/ISBN 978-0-545-62395-7 (paperback)

10

17 18/0

Printed in the U.S.A.

23

First Scholastic printing, September 2014
Book Design by Will Denton
Edited by Katie Carella

INTO THE GRAVEYARD

"Come on. This will just take a minute," said Sam to his friends, Antonio and Lucy. It was Monday morning before school. They were standing outside the entrance to the town graveyard, Eerie Cemetery.

"Sam, do we really have to do this?" Lucy asked. "I've got the willies, big time."

"Me, too," Antonio said. "I'm allergic to graveyards."

Sam Graves turned to his friends. "We need to figure out how to stop our evil school, right?" he said. "Then we *have* to do this. We have to learn as much about Eerie Elementary as possible. That way, we'll be able to fight it!"

The three friends stepped through the iron gate. The graveyard usually gave Sam the creeps, but it didn't seem so scary now — not after everything that had happened. . . .

It was one week ago that Mr. Nekobi, the old man who took care of Eerie Elementary, had chosen Sam to be the new hall monitor.

Years ago, Mr. Nekobi had been the school's hall monitor. He showed Sam the truth about Eerie Elementary: It was alive! The school was a living, breathing, *evil* thing.

Then, on Friday, the school had tried to *swallow* Lucy and Antonio during the class play! Sam had saved them in the nick of time. The three friends and Mr. Nekobi were the only ones who knew the truth about the school. They had to keep everyone safe.

"There!" Lucy said, pointing to a hill dotted with cracked headstones. "The book says that's where the Eerie family is buried."

Lucy held a thick and dusty book in her hands: *Eerie: A Town History.*

The three friends had spent the weekend at the town library looking for information. From this book, they learned that a family with the last name of *Eerie* started the town hundreds of years ago. The book said that the Eerie family was buried in this graveyard. It also said that each member of the Eerie family had started part of the town — the library, the hospital, and even the school! Sam hoped that by seeing the graves they might learn more about the school's history.

Sam eyed the headstones. Each headstone had the name *Eerie* on it. It felt as if the headstones were watching him. Sam counted them: twelve. "Lucy, can I see the book?" Sam asked.

Lucy handed it to Sam. He flipped through the pages. "Guys, this is strange," he said. "The book says there were thirteen members of the Eerie family. So there should be thirteen headstones. But there are only twelve. One family member is *not* buried here."

"Weird . . ." Antonio said. "You know, it's no surprise all this creepy stuff is happening in a town named Eerie — 'eerie' *does* mean spooky and strange."

"Whose grave is missing, Sam?" Lucy asked.

Sam's eyes darted over the names on the headstones. Then he looked in the book.

"Well," Sam said. "There's a family member named Orson Eerie. See his picture here?"

Antonio peeked over Sam's shoulder. "Wow! Look at his mustache!" he said. "What *is* that thing?!"

Sam rolled his eyes and continued, "But I don't see a headstone with that name. And this is even weirder! Orson Eerie was born in 1871, but it doesn't say when he died. There's just a question mark."

"I wonder what happened to him," Antonio said. "What else does the book say about him?"

Sam turned the page to read more.

"OH, NO!" Lucy yelled. "It's 8:15! We're late for school!" Lucy yanked the book from Sam's hands. She stuffed it into her backpack.

"Come on!" Antonio said to Sam.

Sam ran after his friends. But he had an uneasy feeling in his stomach. As hall monitor, Sam could sense things that other students couldn't. He could *feel* when something was wrong at Eerie Elementary. And right now, Sam had the feeling that something very bad was about to happen.

GONE!

Sam raced out of the graveyard, down the street, and toward the school. As the three friends crossed the playground, they spotted a large plastic thermometer on a tree branch.

"I forgot!" Lucy called to her friends as she ran. "We have that weather lesson today!"

Antonio started skipping. "Class outside! This is going to be a good day."

Sam hoped Antonio was right.

The three of them raced up the steps and into the school. Sam pulled on his hall monitor sash as they ran inside. "I'll never get used to wearing this ugly thing," said Sam.

"Bright orange is totally your color!" joked Lucy.

Their classmates were all lined up in the hallway. Ms. Grinker, their teacher, stood at the front of the line. "You're late!" Ms. Grinker barked. "Put away your backpacks and head to the back of the line."

As Sam and his friends walked to their lockers, Ms. Grinker called out, "We're going outside for our weather lesson now. Today's weather will be the hottest ever for late September — 105 degrees!"

Sam and Antonio put their backpacks away quickly. But Lucy was still at her locker. "Just one second!" Lucy said, digging through her backpack. "I need my sunglasses."

"Hurry up, Lucy!" Sam said. He and Antonio hopped into line.

"Hall monitor!" Ms. Grinker called to Sam from the front of the line. "Please make sure everyone is with us."

"Okay," Sam said. He turned to call Lucy, but when he looked down the hall, his heart just about stopped. Lucy's sunglasses lay on the floor. Her locker was open. The hallway was empty.

A feeling of fear crept over Sam. . . .

Lucy was gone.

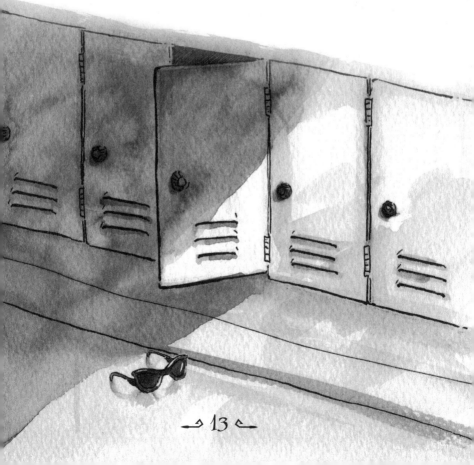

INTO THE LOCKER

Sam had a pit in his stomach the size of a basketball. Last week, Mr. Nekobi had told him that Eerie Elementary fed on students. And Sam had seen this with his own eyes — when the stage had tried to *swallow* his friends. Now Lucy was missing! Could the school have eaten her?

"Follow me!" Ms. Grinker called out. Then she began marching the students out through the big double doors. Sam grabbed Antonio from the end of the line.

The two friends stayed behind as their classmates headed outside. Then Sam said, "Lucy's missing! She went to her locker and now she's gone!"

Antonio turned to look at Lucy's locker. He, too, knew what horrible things Eerie Elementary could do. He gulped and said, "Maybe she's just messing with us. You know, hiding in her locker . . ."

Sam and Antonio crept toward Lucy's locker. Sam's heart pounded. He wrapped his fingers around the half-open door. The metal felt warm in his hand. Sam held his breath. Then he yanked the door open.

Lucy was not inside.

But something else was: Nasty, slimy goo dripped down the inside of the locker. It was glowing. It looked like neon boogers mixed with bulldog slobber.

Antonio touched it. It was sticky and wet. *"Eww!"* he said. He flicked his hand, splashing goo on the floor.

"Antonio," Sam said slowly, "the locker ate Lucy!"

"We should tell Mr. Nekobi!" Antonio said.

Sam shook his head. "There's no time. I have to go in after her. I'm the hall monitor. It's my job to protect the students — *especially Lucy!*"

Antonio gulped. "Then I'm coming with you."

Sam nodded. He reached into Lucy's locker and brushed aside her gym clothes. There was a strange hole in the back wall of the locker. More glowing goo dripped from the hole. Sam could see a narrow tunnel through the hole.

"Are you ready?" Sam asked.

Antonio shook his head. "Not really."

Sam swallowed. "No time to be scared," he said. "It's time to rescue Lucy."

Sam climbed through the hole. Antonio followed. Together, they crawled into the darkness, down into the depths of the school.

A TIGHT SPOT

4

Sam soon saw that the dark tunnel they were crawling through was actually an air vent. It carried cool air into the classrooms. Sam shivered — partly from the cool air and partly from fear.

As they crawled, the inside of the air vent became wetter. Slimy goo dripped down the sides. "It feels like we're crawling through someone's nose!" Antonio said.

Each time Sam placed his hand down, it made a slushy sound.

"I just wish it wasn't so dark," Sam said.

CLİCK!

A light shone in the tunnel. Sam craned his neck and saw Antonio holding a cell phone. Antonio grinned. "My mom makes me carry it."

"Smart!" Sam said.

They crawled forward through the muck. "So, why do you think the school took Lucy?" Antonio asked.

"*Shhh!*" Sam said, whispering.

"We don't want the school to know we're coming."

"I'll be very extra qui —" Antonio started, but then —

"AHH-CHOOO!"

"Antonio!" Sam moaned.

"I'm sorry! It's hard to breathe with your stinky sneakers in my face!"

SWOOSH! A wave of air whooshed through the vent, blowing back Sam's hair. But this air was warm. It felt like someone's hot breath!

"The school must be trying to figure out where we are," Sam whispered. "So don't make

a- a- a- a-"

AHH-CHOOo!

This time it was Sam who sneezed.

"Sam!" Antonio said.

"Sorry!"

KLANG!

Sam looked behind them. Lucy's locker door slammed shut! The school definitely knew where they were. And now they were trapped. No turning back.

All of the sudden, the vent began to shake. The metal buckled. It began to squeeze them!

"We have to get out of here!" Sam said.

The vent squeezed tighter, closing around them! It pressed against Sam's shoulders. It pressed against his legs. Sam and Antonio crawled forward as fast as they could.

The vent squeezed them harder.

"It's going to crush us!" Antonio screamed.

LUNCHTIME

5

The vent was tightening fast. Both boys struggled to move. When Sam placed his hand down, he almost tumbled forward. There was nothing there! Just air! The vent came to a sudden end.

Well, anything is better than being crushed! Sam thought.

"Follow me," Sam said. "And get ready for a drop!"

Sam wriggled forward. Then he was falling.

"*AHHH!!*" Sam screamed as he tumbled through the air.

SPLAT!

Sam splashed down on something gooey.

"Heads up!" Antonio shouted. He was nose-diving toward Sam.

POW!

Antonio plowed into Sam.

It was pitch-black. Antonio turned on his phone again and shone the light around. They were lying on a mountain of sticky gunk.

"It looks like the nasty goo saved us!" Antonio said as he wiped some from his face. "But where are we?" Even with the light from the phone, they couldn't see far ahead.

Sam squinted. They were in a large room. There were tall pillars around the sides of the room and piles of junk all over the floor. The air felt damp. It smelled moldy.

"We must be in the basement," Sam said, getting to his feet. He was covered in goo. His sneakers made squishy sounds with every step.

Then Sam heard a different noise. The boys turned toward it.

An old lunch cart was coming out of the darkness. Its wheels squeaked, echoing against the basement walls. It weaved slowly from side to side.

Goose bumps covered Sam's skin. Antonio inched closer to Sam.

No one was pushing the lunch cart.

It was moving on its own.

The lid opened and closed.

CLICK CLACK! CLICK CLACK! CLICK CLACK!

The lid snapped like a mouth as it rolled toward them. And it wasn't stopping!

"We're about to become school lunch!" yelled Sam.

THE DARK
BASEMENT

6

Sweat poured down Sam's forehead. He had never been so scared in his life. The lunch cart rolled toward him and Antonio. Then, just as it was about to hit them, the boys jumped out of the way.

SLAM!

The cart crashed so hard into the wall it shattered! Pieces of plastic showered Sam and Antonio.

Antonio's jaw hung open. "Um, Sam . . . Maybe we should go back . . . to get help," he said.

Sam shook his head. He knew that the school was trying to scare them into giving up. But he was not going to let that happen. Lucy was counting on them.

Besides, he knew they must have fallen twenty feet from the vent before they landed in that pile of goo. He didn't know how they would *ever* get out of this basement.

Sam turned to his friend. "Antonio, we are deep inside the school now! I bet even Mr. Nekobi never made it this far. This is our chance to learn the secret of Eerie Elementary. If we can figure out what keeps it alive, we can learn how to beat it!" Sam said.

"But, Sam —"

"And we *must* rescue Lucy!" Sam continued.

Antonio swallowed. "You're right."

Sam and Antonio began tiptoeing across the basement. Their hearts were pounding. Antonio shone the light as they walked. Goo ran down the walls. It dripped from the ceiling. Torn-up jackets and shredded backpacks lay across the floor. Bent and twisted bicycles lay in heaps. Everything looked like it had been chewed up.

It was like they were inside a body. And Sam thought that if Eerie Elementary was a body, then this basement must be its stomach.

Sam looked around and said, "It looks like the school has just been eating backpacks and bicycles and stuff. Mr. Nekobi really *has* done a good job of protecting the students."

"You've done great, too!" Antonio said. "If you hadn't saved us at the class play last Friday, *I'd* be down here!"

"Come on, let's finish this," said Sam.

The friends tiptoed along. Then Antonio grabbed Sam's arm.

"Look!" Antonio said, pointing.

"What?" Sam asked. He followed Antonio's beam of light over toward a rusty metal desk.

"It's him. It's Orson Eerie!" Antonio yelled.

THE FACE OF ORSON EERIE

7

Antonio was shining the light at a picture frame on the desk. Inside, there was an old black-and-white photo of a man.

"Geez, Antonio!" Sam said. "You scared me! I thought you meant Orson Eerie was *here*! Like, real, back to life, in person!"

Sam felt around on the wall until he found a light switch. He flipped it on.

Two light bulbs flickered on.

The light was dim, but Sam could see that this corner of the basement was a sort of office. There were charts hanging from the walls and papers on the desk. Everything was covered in a thick layer of dust.

The boys stepped closer to the desk. Sam picked up the picture frame. "You're right," Sam said. "Look at the glasses and the creepy mustache. This is Orson Eerie!"

"I don't think anyone has been here in a long, long time," Antonio said, picking up a newspaper. "This is from 1938! That's older than my grandmother! That's older than, like, my grandmother's grandmother!"

"Whoa," said Sam. "And what is this?" A large piece of blue paper lay out on the desk.

"It looks like a blueprint," Antonio said. "Like a drawing of a building."

"That makes sense. This big room looks like our gym. See?" said Sam, pointing to the blueprint. "It's like a map of Eerie Elementary."

Suddenly, a girl's voice called out, "HELP!"

"Lucy!" Sam and Antonio said at once.

Lucy's cries were coming from beyond a large metal door. It was at the far end of the dark basement. A sign on the door read HEATING AND COOLING ROOM.

"Let's go!" Sam said.

The boys quickly stuffed everything they could fit into their pockets: papers, a small book, and the blueprint. But as soon as they did, *everything* in the basement came to life!

WHOOSH! A dodge ball flew at Sam. Sam grabbed Antonio by the wrist. "Come on!" Sam shouted, ducking beneath the ball. "Let's go get Lucy!"

Sam dodged chewed-up Frisbees that rocketed toward him! Antonio jumped over roller skates that shot toward his legs like cannonballs!

BRRRGGLLL!!!!

The school was *loud*! Sam thought it sounded like a stomach rumbling! The walls shook and the floors shifted! Sam and Antonio stumbled from side to side. Backpacks opened wide and threw rulers, pencils, and books at them.

The Heating and Cooling Room door was just ahead. "Keep running!" Sam yelled.

But Antonio stopped in his tracks. Sam looked back. Something long that looked like a spear was headed for Antonio. A whiffle ball bat!

Sam pulled Antonio behind a large pillar.

WHOOSH!

The bat flew past.

"Okay, *now* I'm mad,"
Antonio said. "Let's find
Lucy and get out of this
crazy basement!"

Sam peeked
around the pillar.
"We just need to
reach that door."

"But who knows
what's waiting for us
on the other side?"
asked Antonio.

"There's only one way
to find out," said Sam.

LUCY!

8

Sam and Antonio charged toward the Heating and Cooling Room. Sam ripped the door open, then quickly shut it behind them.

CRASH! A hundred mad chewed-up things slammed into the closed door.

Sam caught his breath and looked around the room.

One wall was covered with a maze of rusty old pipes. The pipes were alive! They moved like an army of snakes. As they twisted, they scraped together, making a screeching noise.

"Lucy!" Sam yelled, pointing. His friend was suspended in midair, hanging upside down. One of the pipes was wrapped around her ankle.

"Guys! You found me! Please get me down from here!" Lucy shrieked.

Lucy calling for help made the school angrier. The pipe around Lucy's ankle began flinging her through the air.

"That pipe is throwing Lucy around like a doll!" said Antonio.

"Hang on, Lucy!" Sam yelled.

Sam and Antonio began climbing the giant wall of pipes. Unlike the basement, this room was not covered in goo. The metal pipes were dry, and the boys were able to grip them. Sam could feel water rushing through the pipes. *These pipes must pump water throughout the school,* thought Sam.

Antonio leapt off one pipe and grabbed the pipe around Lucy's right ankle. He tugged, trying to pull her free.

"I'm coming!" said Sam.

"The pipe is wrapped so tight!" Antonio yelled, as he tugged.

"HELP!" Lucy cried.

Antonio pulled harder, but then —

KLANK!

The pipe jumped in his hand, throwing him to the ground. *"Argh!"* Antonio said, getting to his feet. "It's no use!"

Sam jumped down. *There has to be a way to make that pipe let go of her,* he thought. He looked around the room. The school's water heater stood in the corner. Sam's dad was a plumber, so Sam knew all about this stuff. This water heater warmed the water. Then it pumped the warm water throughout the school. A wheel on the front controlled how fast the water moved through the pipes. *If I turn that wheel, I can slow down*  *the water! Maybe that will weaken the pipes and make them let go of Lucy,* Sam thought.

Sam grabbed the wheel. It was rusty and stiff. Finally, it started turning. But it wasn't helping. Lucy was flung around faster!

"What are you doing, Sam?!" yelled Antonio.

"STOP! You're making it worse!" Lucy screamed.

She was being whipped through the air at lightning speed. Faster and faster! Sam had to free his friend before it was too late!

THE HORRIBLE TRUTH

The he school kept flinging Lucy through the air. Back and forth. Back and forth. Sam got an idea: *I must be turning the wheel the wrong way!*

"Hang on!" he shouted.

Sam spun the big wheel in the opposite direction. The water began draining from the pipes. It was working! The pipes were losing their energy. They were becoming weaker. Then the pipe around Lucy's ankle loosened its grip. And it dropped her!

"*Ahhhhhhhh!*" yelled Lucy, falling.

At the last moment, Lucy grabbed ahold of a lower-hanging pipe. Antonio helped her get down. "You're okay," Antonio said.

Lucy wiped some sweat from her forehead. "So," she said, "what took you guys so long?"

Sam and Antonio smiled. Their friend was safe.

"What is all that?" Lucy said, pointing to the papers sticking up out of Sam and Antonio's pockets.

"Oh, yeah!" Sam said. "We found this creepy office back there. It was full of lots of old junk!"

"Maybe that blueprint will show us how to get back upstairs," said Antonio.

"Good thinking!" said Lucy. "You find a way out of here while I dig through this other stuff."

Sam, Antonio, and Lucy took a seat on the floor and got to work.

"Look at this!" Lucy said, holding up a red leather book. "This is Orson Eerie's journal. It sounds like he was some sort of mad scientist!"

"Whoa," Antonio whispered.

"What else does his journal say?" Sam asked.

Lucy's eyes darted over the pages. After a minute, she lowered the book and said, "As Orson Eerie grew old, all he cared about was the idea of endless life. In his last journal entry, he writes, *'I've done it! I've found a way to live forever.'*"

Sam remembered something. "Lucy, do you still have the library book?"

Lucy's eyes lit up. "Yes!" she said. She slipped her backpack off her shoulder and handed the book to Sam.

"Look!" Sam said, flipping to the page where he had left off that morning. "It says Orson Eerie was an architect — someone who designs buildings. And, *oh, man* — he designed Eerie Elementary!"

"Wait a minute," said Antonio. "A mad scientist designed our school? No wonder it's crazy creepy!"

Sam, Antonio, and Lucy were silent. The only sound came from the water heater. It sounded like a heart beating.

Ba BUMP, Ba BUMP.
Ba BUMP, Ba BUMP.
Ba BUMP, Ba BUMP.

It was then that Sam Graves understood the terrible truth about Orson Eerie *and* about Eerie Elementary.

TRAPPED!

10

"I get it now!" Sam yelled, holding up the blueprint and the book. "It all makes sense. Orson Eerie designed this school so that he could stay alive forever. That's why we couldn't find a grave for him in the town graveyard! He *never* died! He became the school!"

"Wait," Antonio said. "So you're saying —"

"Orson Eerie *is* Eerie Elementary!" Sam said. "He is the walls and the floors. He is the lockers and the pipes. He is *everything*! That's why the school took *you* this morning, Lucy! It sensed that we found that library book! It knew we were close to finding out the truth!"

Lucy's face went white. "This whole thing... It's terrifying..."

Sam agreed. It was almost too crazy to believe! But it *did* make sense. It explained everything.

CLACK!

The lock on the Heating and Cooling Room door slid into place, trapping them!

Then Eerie Elementary started going *crazy*. The walls began to vibrate! The pipes began shaking and clanking again! And the floor cracked open!

The friends stumbled back.

"What's happening?!" Lucy screamed.

"Now that we've uncovered its secret," Sam yelled, "the school will *never* let us out!"

Antonio jumped back. "My feet are getting *wet*!"

Water bubbled up through the crack in the floor. It was rising up fast.

"We don't have much time!" Sam yelled. The water was over his sneakers.

Lucy yanked on the door handle, but it wouldn't unlock. "We're stuck!" Sam gulped.

The water rushed up through the floor *fast*. It was already above their knees. And there was no way out.

SLIPPERY ESCAPE

11

The three friends kicked their feet to stay above water. Soon, they'd touch the ceiling! The water would fill the entire room.

KLANG!

BANG!

KLONK!

The pipes were banging loudly. Sam could barely think.

"Wait! These pipes go all throughout the school!" said Sam. He pointed at one big pipe. It was broken. "Guys, climb inside that big pipe! I've got an idea!"

"Are you crazy?!" Lucy yelled.

Antonio shook his head. "No way. I'm not climbing into that old pipe! We don't know where it will take us! And I don't want to get squeezed again!"

"It's our only choice!" Sam said.

Antonio looked at Sam, then groaned. "Fine!" He swam over to the largest pipe. It was the size of a giant water slide. He climbed in. Sam helped Lucy up into the big pipe, too. The dark water was still rising. Sam needed to hurry. "I'll be right back!"

"Where are you going?!" Lucy shouted.

"Trust me!" Sam said.

Sam took one deep breath and dove down. For once, he was actually thankful for all of those swim classes his mom had made him take.

Sam opened his eyes as he reached the water heater. Earlier, he had turned the wheel to the right to lessen the water's strength and save Lucy. So if he turned it to the left, it should make the water move faster through the pipes.

If the water is stronger, it can push us through the pipes! The water can carry us to the other end of the pipes, hopefully above ground, thought Sam.

It was a crazy idea, but it was their only chance.

Sam grabbed ahold of the wheel
and began turning.

DEAD END

Sam was having trouble turning the giant wheel under water. And he was running out of air!

If this plan doesn't work, my friends and I are in serious trouble! he thought. Sam pictured Lucy and Antonio and Mr. Nekobi. He pictured Ms. Grinker and all of his classmates. Eerie Elementary put them all in danger, and only he could save them. He was the hall monitor. He could feel the school. And he sensed now that he could beat the school! If only he could turn the wheel!

He could not fail.

He would not fail!

Sam used all his strength to give the wheel another tug.

SCREECH!

It worked! The wheel was turning. Then Sam saw a dial atop the water heater, labeled WATER SPEED. *How did I not see that before?* wondered Sam. As he turned the wheel, a small needle on the dial moved from green to red. The word *DANGER* was in the red section.

Sam pressed his feet against the water heater and turned the wheel until the dial's needle was past the word *DANGER*. The water heater began shaking!

It's going to blow!
Sam thought. *I've got to get out of here!*

Sam turned and kicked with all of his might. He burst through the surface and gasped for breath.

Antonio and Lucy were inside the pipe, waiting for him. Water rushed faster and faster through the pipes. All around Sam, the water was bubbling and splashing. The water heater shook.

"Sam, what did you do?!" Antonio yelled.

"I'm getting us out of here! We'll travel through the pipes!" Sam said.

"I hope this works!" Lucy said, sticking out a hand. Sam grabbed ahold, and Lucy pulled him up.

He lay down behind Antonio and Lucy inside the big pipe. It was like the three of them were lying at the top of a water slide. But they weren't going on a fun zip *down* into a swimming pool. No — they were going to be rocketed, *up, through Eerie Elementary!*

"Where will this pipe spit us out?" Lucy asked.

Sam didn't answer. He had *no idea* where this pipe would take them. He just hoped it was somewhere above ground.

The pipe started really shaking. The water heater would *blow* at any moment and water would be *blasted through the pipe*!

"Hold your breath!" Sam shouted. "Here we go —"

BOOM!

The water heater blew! There was a giant blast of warm water! Sam, Antonio, and Lucy were *launched* through the pipe.

VA-ZOOM!

The three friends raced through the pipe at 100 miles per hour on a wave of water.

Up ahead, the pipe split into two. Lucy shouted, *"Sammmmmmmm!!!!"*

As the pipes split, Lucy was carried off in one direction, and Sam and Antonio went in another.

Sam held his breath as he zoomed through the pipe. Up ahead, the pipe split into two again. The water carried Antonio to the right. Sam tried to follow him, but it was too late.

Sam whizzed down a different pipe. Now Sam Graves was all alone, flying through Eerie Elementary!

Sam saw darkness at the end of the pipe.

Oh, no.

It was a dead end!

He had to slow down or he would smash into the end of the pipe. He reached out and scraped his fingers against the pipe. But it was no use.

He couldn't stop! He couldn't slow down!

HANGING BY A THREAD

13

I need to do something, or I'll be smashed! Sam thought. He lay flat as a board. He pushed his feet forward as the water rocketed him toward the end of the pipe. *My sneakers and this fast speed just have to help me break through this old rusty pipe!*

Sam's feet slammed into the end of the pipe.

CRASH!

It cracked open! Sam was *shot out* into the air.

"Oh, no!" he screamed. He was high above the lunchroom.

He was in midair!

Thirty feet up!

And then falling!

Sam reached out for something, anything to stop his fall. He grabbed on to one of the huge curtains that covered the room's floor-to-ceiling windows.

Sam looked up at the pipe end above him. Gallons of water were pouring out of the pipe and splashing to the floor below.

But then the flow of water began to slow.

The water heater must have run out of water. The danger was over!

I did it! Sam thought, dangling from the curtain. He looked down. The lunchroom was empty. *Phew! I'll just climb down this curtain. Then I'll find Antonio and Lucy.*

But no!

Eerie Elementary was not done with Sam Graves! The water on the lunchroom floor began rising. It was taking shape. It was becoming *something*.

Sam gasped.

The water was taking the form of *a giant hand*.

"Help!" Sam shouted. He tried to climb higher up the curtain, but the curtain began swaying! It was trying to shake Sam off! The curtain had come to life!

RIP!

The curtain started to tear! Sam looked down at the huge watery hand of Eerie Elementary. It opened wide. It was reaching for him!

WATERY HAND

Sam hung by a thread from the monstrous curtain. He was about to be grabbed by the enormous hand. But wait! Sam remembered something. That morning, Ms. Grinker had said, "Today's weather will be the hottest ever."

Sam tightened his grip on the curtain, and then he tugged! The curtain tore. The entire curtain fell to the ground — along with Sam.

Sunlight poured through the window. Hot rays of sunlight were shining directly on the watery hand.

The hand pulled back as though it were in pain. Steam started rising off of it. The sun's heat was turning the water into steam! The school howled!

But still, the hand reached for Sam. It was hurt, weakened — but not beaten.

If I could just bring down the other curtains in here, the sunlight would destroy the hand, thought Sam. *But I'm cornered.*

Watery fingers were about to grab Sam.

Lucy and Antonio burst into the lunchroom. "We're coming, Sam!" they yelled.

"Pull down those curtains!" Sam shouted. "Quick!"

Antonio and Lucy didn't know what Sam's plan was, but they trusted him. Antonio tugged on one curtain! Lucy grabbed another! Soon, even more sunlight flooded the room!

The watery hand was almost beaten! Sam just needed to deliver the final blow. He spotted a metal cooking tray on the floor.

Metal reflects light! thought Sam.

Sam stepped on the edge of the tray, popping it up into the air like a skateboard. He snatched it and held it up to the sunlight. A white-hot beam of light bounced off the metal, toward the hand.

HISSSS!!!!

The hand of Eerie Elementary screamed!

It shook! Steam clouded the air. And then —

BOOM-SPLASH!

The watery hand blew apart! Giant drops
of water splashed across the room.
The hand was gone. It was done.

Sam got to his feet.

Then he said, "You guys got here just in time! Where were you?"

"The pipe spit me out over in the gym," Lucy said.

"And I got spit out into the fifth-grade hallway," Antonio said. "Luckily, no one saw us!"

Sam was so tired he could barely stand.

"Man, I owe you guys big time!" said Sam.

"Are you kidding?! You two saved *me* today!" Lucy said.

"It was *all* Sam," said Antonio. He began clapping. "Sam Graves, hall monitor hero! Give him a hand!"

Sam groaned. "I never want to hear the word *hand* again." The friends smiled.

They were safe.

But not for long.

SLAM!

The door flew open. Ms. Grinker burst into the lunchroom. She looked around, eyes wide. Her frizzy hair was standing on end. "Sam! Antonio! Lucy! Where have you been?!" she yelled. "What happened to the curtains? Why is everything wet?!"

Just then, Mr. Nekobi rushed in. He began calmly mopping up the water. Then he said, "Ms. Grinker, Sam was helping me wash the windows. Didn't I tell you?"

Ms. Grinker was still upset. "No! You didn't tell me! And Sam should've asked me if he could leave class. He missed our entire weather lesson."

"I'm becoming forgetful in my old age," Mr. Nekobi said. Sam smiled and looked to the floor. Mr. Nekobi to the rescue!

"What about Antonio and Lucy?" Ms. Grinker said. "They're not hall monitors so *they* shouldn't be helping you."

"I'm making them assistant hall monitors. They've proven to be very helpful to Sam."

Antonio and Lucy looked at each other with big, excited smiles.

Ms. Grinker was mad. She turned on her heels and stomped out of the lunchroom.

As soon as Ms. Grinker and the other students left, Sam told Mr. Nekobi *everything*.

"You've learned a lot about the school," Mr. Nekobi said. "And you seriously hurt the school this time. Hopefully, the evil will stay asleep for a while."

"And hopefully assistant hall monitors don't have to wear these ugly things!" Lucy said. She tugged on Sam's bright orange sash.

"Hey!" Sam said. Soon all four of them were laughing.

After school that day, Sam, Lucy, and Antonio sat on the swings.

"We did well today," Sam said. "But I don't think we'll *ever* be able to *really* defeat Eerie Elementary."

Lucy hopped down off her swing. "I don't think that's true," she said.

Antonio nodded. "We're a team. And now we know Orson Eerie *is* the school. There must be a way we can undo whatever he did."

Sam stared at the school building: Eerie Elementary, the strange creation that *was* mad scientist Orson Eerie.

"You guys are right," he said. "There must be a way to beat Eerie Elementary, once and for all. And, together, *we* will find it!"

Shhhh!

This news is top secret:

Jack Chabert is a pen name for Max Brallier. (Max uses a made-up name instead of his real name so Orson Eerie won't come after him, too!)

Max was once a hall monitor at Joshua Eaton Elementary School in Reading, MA. But today, Max lives in a weird, old apartment building in New York City. His days are spent writing, playing video games, and reading comic books. And at night, he walks the halls, always prepared for the moment when his building will come alive.

Max is the author of more than twenty books for children, including the middle-grade series The Last Kids on Earth and Galactic Hot Dogs.

Sam Ricks went to a haunted elementary school, but he never got to be the hall monitor. As far as Sam knows, the school never tried to eat him. Sam graduated from The University of Baltimore with a master's degree in design. During the day, he illustrates from the comfort of his non-carnivorous home. And at night, he reads strange tales to his four children.

HOW MUCH DO YOU KNOW ABOUT

Eerie Elementary

The Locker ATE Lucy?

What do Sam and his friends learn from the book *Eerie: A Town History*?

What is the terrible truth about Orson Eerie and Eerie Elementary?

How does the sun help Sam, Antonio, and Lucy save the day?

Pretend your school comes to life. Use sound-effects words to write an action-packed story.

KLANG!
BOOM!
RUMBLE!

Sam, Lucy, and Antonio visit the library to research their town. Visit your local library to see what interesting **facts** you can uncover about your town!